THE ELEPHANT AND THE TREE

Jin Pyn Lee

RP|KIDS

PHILADELPHIA • LONDON

© 2006, 2009 by Jin Pyn Lee

All rights reserved under the Pan-American and
International Copyright Conventions

First published in Singapore by Epigram Books and Ele Books LLP, 2006

First published in the United States
by Running Press Book Publishers, 2009

Printed in China

9   8   7   6   5   4   3   2   1
Digit on the right indicates the number of this printing

Library of Congress Control Number: 2008933255

ISBN 978-0-7624-3532-6

This edition published by
Running Press Kids, an imprint of
Running Press Book Publishers
2300 Chestnut Street
Philadelphia, PA 19103-4371

Visit us on the web!
www.runningpress.com

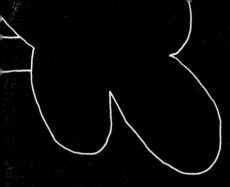

for the voiceless

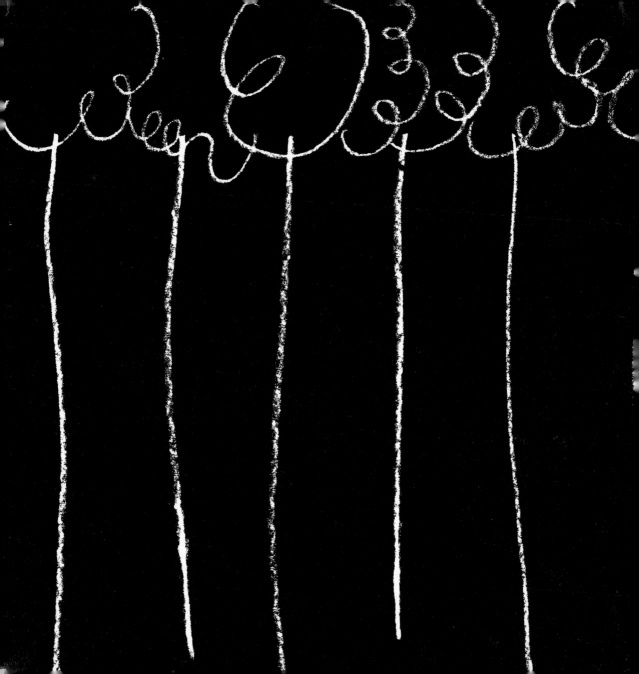

Once there was an elephant
who lived in the forest.

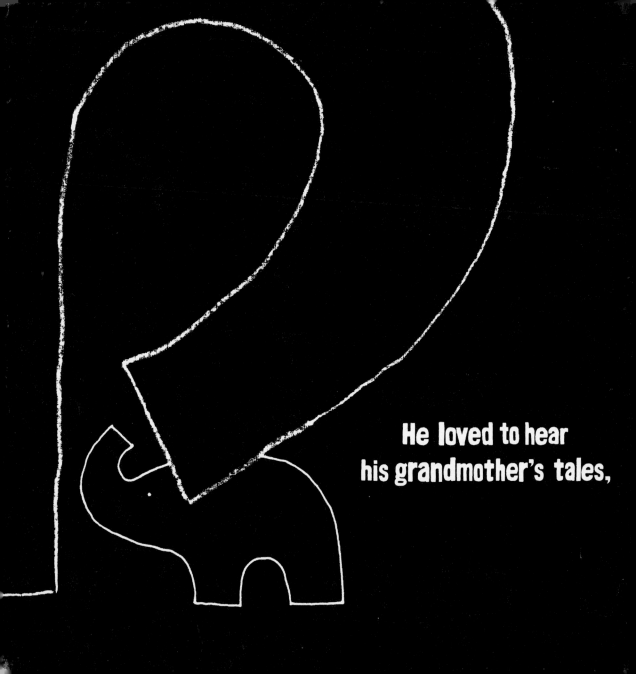

He loved to hear
his grandmother's tales,

he loved to wander free.

To swim in the stream and

smell the jasmine,

to play with

his forest friends.

he always remembered

But wherever the elephant wandered

to return to one single tree.

The tree and the elephant were best of friends,
both were young and both were small.

The elephant loved scratching himself on the tree

and the tree loved wandering with the elephant's stories.

They loved feeling the grass beds

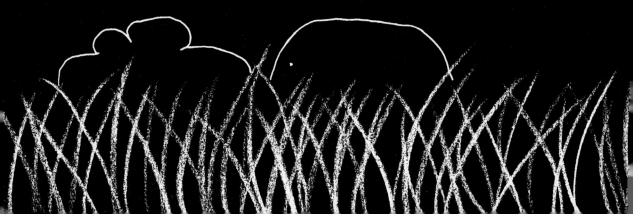

and climbing the cliffs,

the elephant and the tree

were as happy as can be.

As the years passed,

the elephant became big and strong,

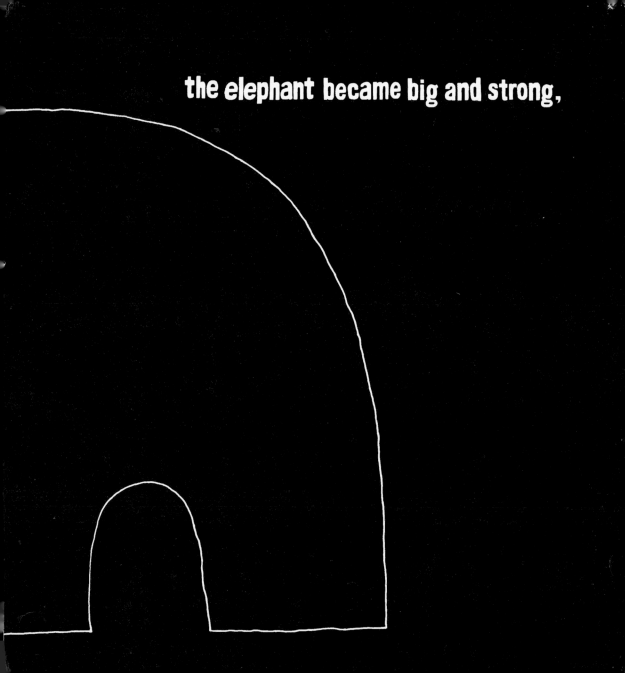

and the tree grew taller and taller than all the other trees.

Now it was the elephant's turn to listen to stories

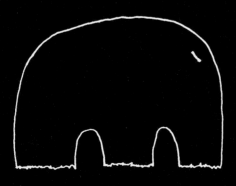

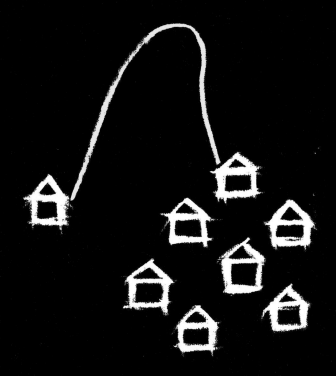

of little people and their houses,
where the elephant's playground used to be.

One day the forest shrilled and shook.
"Run, my friend!" the tree told the elephant,

but the elephant would not move.

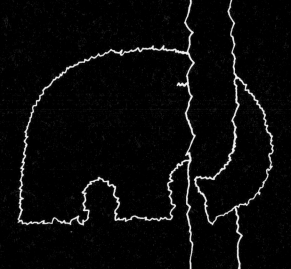

A shot rang out.
The elephant woke in a different land,

no longer free.

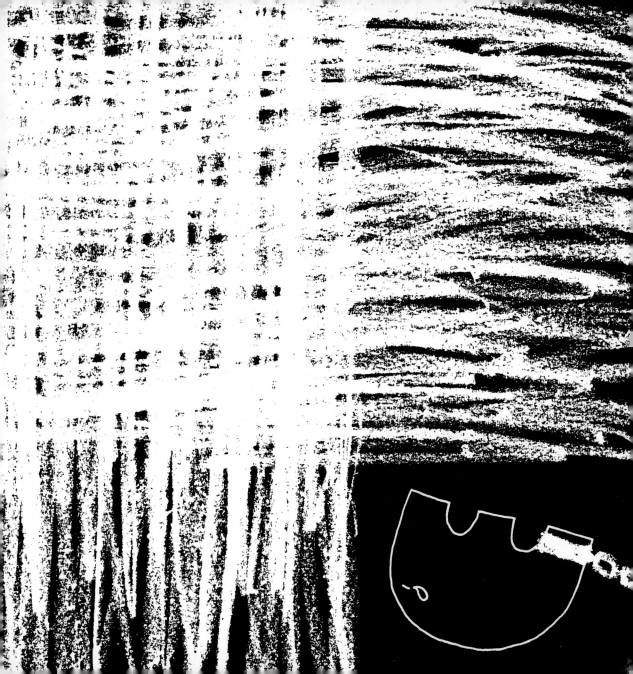

"Ouch!" The elephant groaned
as they placed a hard, heavy load on his back.

"It's me, my friend," said the tree.
"The day you were shot, I was chopped down
and made into an elephant saddle."

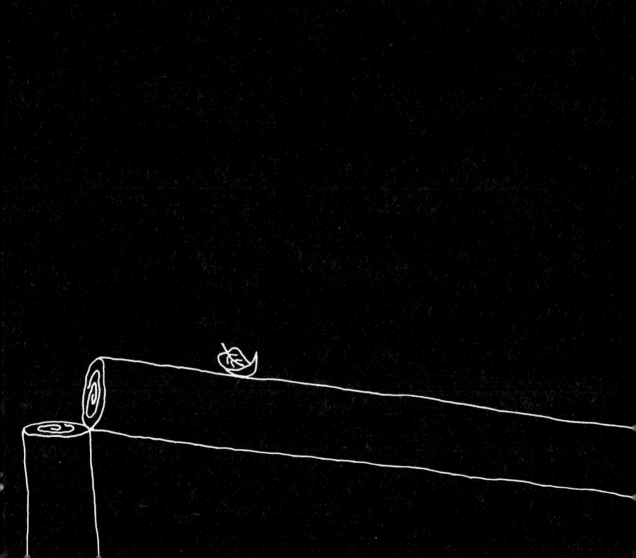

So it was that the two friends stayed together,
one chained and one bound,
recounting their happy memories.

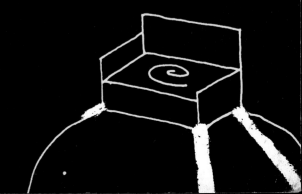

and streams swum,

and grass beds felt,

their days of wandering free.
The elephant and the tree.